# FAVORITE
# MEDIEVAL
# TALES

RETOLD BY
## MARY POPE OSBORNE

ILLUSTRATED BY
## TROY HOWELL

SCHOLASTIC PRESS ⚬ NEW YORK

*Special thanks to David Yerkes, Professor of English and Comparative Literature, Columbia University, for fact checking the manuscript.*

LIBRARY OF CONGRESS CATALOGING-IN-PUBLICATION DATA
Osborne, Mary Pope.
Favorite medieval tales / retold by Mary Pope Osborne; illustrated by Troy Howell.    p.  cm.
Summary: A collection of well-known tales from medieval Europe, including "Beowulf," "The Sword in the Stone," "The Song of Roland," and "Gudren and the Island of the Lost Children."

ISBN 0-590-60042-7

1. Tales, Medieval. [1. Tales, Medieval. 2. Folklore — Europe.] I. Howell, Troy, ill. II. Title. PZ8.1.O803Fav 1998    398.2'094 — DC20    96-17285    CIP    AC
10 9 8 7 6 5 4 3 2 1    8 9/9 0/0 01 02 03

Printed in Singapore                46
First edition, May 1998

The text type was set in Sabon.
The display type was set in Post Medieval.
Troy Howell's paintings were rendered
in acrylics on rag board.
Book design by Marijka Kostiw

To Will Boyce ❧ *M. P. O.*

To David and Rebecca ❧ *T. H.*

. . . SO IS IT WITH THIS RHYME:
IT LIVES DISPERSEDLY IN MANY LANDS,
AND EVERY MINSTREL SINGS IT DIFFERENTLY.


– ALFRED, LORD TENNYSON –

# TABLE OF CONTENTS

# INTRODUCTION

**I**N THE BEGINNING of medieval times in Europe, books did not exist. Most people were unable to read or write. **Nevertheless, there were stories** — stories of heroes and monsters, told by minstrels and poets, that were passed down orally from one generation to the next. These songs and verses were important to the people of that age. They inspired warriors to go into battle. They provided a record of a country's history. And they helped people find meaning in the hardship and cruelty of the times.

Eventually, learned scribes, such as Christian monks and nobles, began to record and illustrate those stories. These magnificent works became known as illuminated manuscripts. Between A.D. 1000 and the mid-1400s, all nine tales in this collection were "captured" in such a manner.

These tales came from Ireland, Britain, Germany, Scandinavia, and France. They show how medieval life in western Europe was a period of horror and wonder, brutality and heroism, savagery and chivalry. It was a time when Christianity blended with pagan worship, and people still believed in hideous monsters, magicians, and spirits. It was a time when heroes rushed to give their lives to protect their king, their fellow warriors, their religion, and their honor. And it was a time when women were either scorned or placed high on pedestals.

As I culled from the large body of medieval literature, I selected the particular tales in this collection simply because I loved them. But as I surveyed my choices, I realized something serendipitous had happened. Lined up in a certain sequence, these tales also tell another story — a story about language. For the medieval period was also a time when the English language changed from the Germanic tongue of Old English to an English very close to that which is spoken today.

The first recorded people to live in the British Isles were the Celts, who spoke a tongue that was the ancestor of Old Welsh and Old Irish, the original language of the tale "Finn MacCoul."

In A.D. 43, the Romans overtook the island of Britain, supplanting the religion, laws, and language of the Celts. The Roman tongue, Latin, was dominant until the fifth century, when Anglo-Saxons from the north lands invaded Britain. The Anglo-Saxons spoke Old English, a name given to several Germanic dialects of the northern invaders. *Beowulf* was the greatest work written in Old English.

Eventually Rome sent Christian missionaries to the Anglo-Saxons. The missionaries converted them to Christianity and encouraged them to write in Latin, the language of Geoffrey of Monmouth's *The History of the Kings of Britain*, from which my retelling of Merlin's early life in "The Sword in the Stone" is derived.

In the ninth century came a new wave of invaders — the Vikings — and words of Old Norse were added to Old English. Old Norse may have been the original language of the German poem *Gudrun*, from which I adapted "Island of the Lost Children."

In 1066, Norman conquerors from France invaded England, and a Norman dialect of French pushed aside Old English and became the language of the English court, and the language of *The Song of Roland* and "The Werewolf."

For several generations, hardly anyone wrote in English; it was mainly the everyday speech of the peasants. However, when England became more nationalistic, the nobles abandoned French and turned back to the English tongue, which by now included a stream of Latin and French words. Thus, Old English evolved into Middle English, the language of *Sir Gawain and the Green Knight*, the ballads of Robin Hood, and "Chanticleer and the Fox."

And from the late Middle English prose style of Sir Thomas Malory's *Le Morte Darthur* (from which "The Sword in the Stone" is also derived) came the beginnings of modern English. In 1485, Malory's book was one of the first to be published in English after the invention of the printing press. With the invention of printing, the age of the handwritten medieval manuscript came to an end, and the new age of the *book* began.

The story of English is the story of how the blending of different cultures brought forth a language richer and deeper than that of its original form. The process continues today, especially in America, where so many different cultures have converged and melted together. In the past few hundred years, as immigrants have streamed in from all over the globe, English has absorbed many new words. African, Native American, and Latin

American peoples, among countless others, have contributed words to English, making it one of the most expressive languages in the world.

To give readers a sense of the evolution of language during and since medieval times, I begin each tale with a quote from a source of the story written in its original tongue. Beneath it is a modern English translation. There are also notes at the end of the book that explain in greater detail the ideas and history of the age.

Try now to imagine yourself sitting in the dappled light of the greenwood or near the fire in a feast hall. Though monsters and enemies haunt the shadows, for the moment you are safe. You are friend to Finn, Beowulf, Arthur, Hagen, Roland, and Robin. All grows quiet, a harp begins to play, and the poet starts his tale. . . .

– MARY POPE OSBORNE –

# Finn MacCoul

"Finn do ainm," ol se "a gilla,
ocus is duit tucad in bradan dia
tomailt, ocus is tu in Find co fir."
– Old Irish –

"Fionn is your name, lad," said
he, "and it is to you that the
salmon was given to eat, and
you are the Fionn truly!"
– English translation –

Long ago near the Boyne River in Ireland, there grew nine magic hazel trees. The nuts of the trees were filled with poetry, and whenever they fell into the water and floated upstream, a giant salmon swallowed them. The salmon became known as the "Salmon of Knowledge," and the people of Ireland believed that the person who ate him would become a great poet.

One day a young boy named Demne wandered the banks of the river in search of the salmon — for in ancient Ireland, any boy who wanted to be a great warrior also had to be a great poet.

Demne had not gone far when he came upon an old sooth-sayer named Finn the Seer.

An ancient prophecy said that a person named "Finn" would someday eat the salmon and thus possess all the poetry of the hazel trees. For this reason Finn the Seer had lived for seven years on the riverbank, trying to catch the precious fish.

When the seer met Demne, he hired him as his servant. Shortly thereafter, the seer caught the Salmon of Knowledge. He gave the fish to Demne and said, "Please cook this for me, but whatever you do, do not eat any of the fish yourself."

After the salmon had been cooked, Demne brought the fish to the seer. The boy sucked his thumb as he gave the salmon to the old man.

"Did you eat some?" the seer asked suspiciously.

"No," said the boy.

"Then why do you suck your thumb?"

"I burnt my thumb on the salmon's hot skin. And to ease the pain, I pressed it against the roof of my mouth."

"You scamp!" cried Finn the Seer when he saw the sign of a poet in the boy's eye. "I thought you said your name was Demne. Do you have another name?"

"I do," said the boy. "It's Finn MacCoul."

"Oh," said the seer with great sadness. "So *you* are the Finn who was prophesied to eat this fish. Not me. Go on, my boy, you may eat all you like."

So Finn MacCoul ate the Salmon of Knowledge, and from that day on, he possessed all the poetry of the magic hazel trees.

SOME YEARS LATER, when Finn MacCoul was a young man, he slayed a wicked wizard. For this brave feat, the high king of Ireland made Finn commander of the Fianna, a roving band of the country's greatest warriors and hunters. No man was taken into the Fianna unless he was a prime poet.

One day while Finn and the Fianna were returning from a hunt, they came upon a lovely doe in a meadow.

The hunters dashed after her with their dogs. But the graceful animal ran so fast that soon all the men gave up, except Finn and his two magnificent hounds.

When the doe entered a deep valley, she lay in the tall grass and waited for Finn to catch up to her.

His hounds ran ahead of him, but to Finn's amazement, they did not harm the doe. They merely licked her face and played with her.

HE TVRNED ME
INTO A DOE

The doe then followed Finn and his hounds back to the land of the Fianna warriors. She ran with the two dogs, until they arrived at Finn's house. Then she disappeared, and Finn saw her no more.

Late that night, as Finn sat before his hearth, a beautiful young woman entered his home.

"Who are you?" he said.

"My name is Saba. I was the doe who followed you here," she said. "Three years ago, I refused the love of the Dark Druid. To punish me, he turned me into a doe, and I was forced to live with the wild deer."

Finn was astonished. "How did you change back into a woman?" he asked.

"A good Druid took pity on me," she said. "He promised to release me from the spell once I had arrived in the realm of the Fianna warriors. Your hounds understood my true nature at once and allowed me to follow you here."

So great was Finn's admiration for Saba that he married her. And so great was his love for her that he gave up hunting and riding with the Fianna. He only wanted to be with his wife.

One day, however, invaders attacked the shores of Ireland, forcing Finn to leave Saba and join his men in battle. Being away from Saba was too much for Finn. After seven days, his desire to embrace her overwhelmed him, and he rushed back home.

But inside his house, his joy turned to shock when he found no sign of Saba anywhere. He ran outside and called to her, but instead found his friends and neighbors surrounding his gate, their faces betraying their sorrow.

"Where is my wife?" pleaded Finn.

A gnarled old woman stepped forward. "While you were away, Saba ran to meet you as you came from the fields with your hounds. You stretched out your arms to embrace her. . . ."

"What are you saying?" Finn whispered.

"Your wife ran to you," another neighbor continued. "No sooner did she touch you than did she utter a cry. A moment later, a doe stood in her place."

"Did no one try to save her?" Finn cried.

"Three times she tried to run back to your gate, but each time your hounds chased her away," a neighbor said.

"We ran after her," said another neighbor. "But she vanished! We could hear the tread of her hooves on the grass. But we saw nothing."

Finn fell to his knees and covered his face. He knew at once Saba had been tricked again by the Dark Druid. Overcome with grief, Finn stumbled into his house, and no one saw him until the sun rose on the morrow.

FOR THE NEXT SEVEN YEARS, Finn MacCoul searched the land for his beloved Saba. Then one day, while he and his men hunted, their hounds began to bark wildly.

The hunters followed the fierce sounds into a narrow glen. There they found Finn's two dogs keeping the others at bay.

When Finn drew close, he saw his dogs were guarding a small figure — a dirt-smeared boy with long, matted hair. Finn's two hounds whined and licked the boy as if he were their long-forgotten master.

Finn led the wild child to his hunting cabin, gave him food

and drink, and let him rest. The dogs adored the boy and would not leave his side.

As Finn studied the sleeping child, he noticed a strong resemblance to Saba, his long-lost wife. He woke the boy at once and asked him where he had come from.

The boy told Finn that he had roamed the countryside with a lovely, kind doe. Together, they had lived in the hills and valleys, eating berries and nuts, until one day she had led him to the glen where the men always hunted. She nuzzled him tenderly, as though she were saying good-bye forever, and then she left him.

Now Finn knew for certain that the child was his son, and the grief he had borne all those years turned at once to joy.

Finn named his beloved son Oisin, which means "fawn." And Oisin, like Finn, grew up to be one of ancient Ireland's greatest poets and heroes.

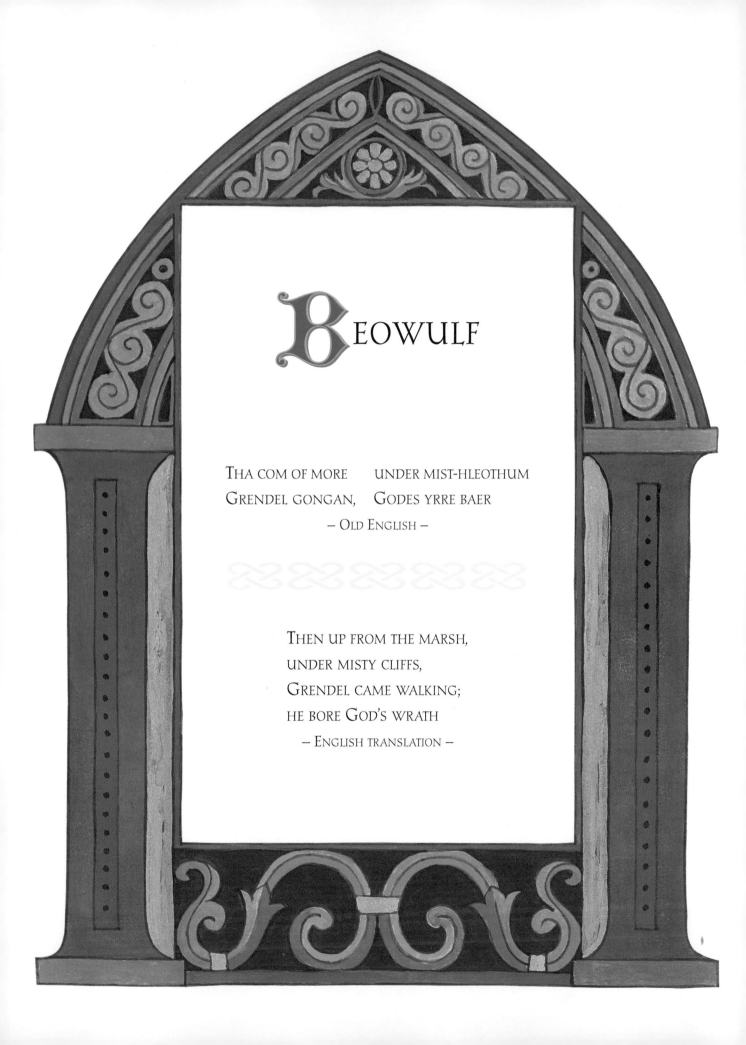

# Beowulf

Tha com of more     under mist-hleothum
Grendel gongan,    Godes yrre baer
— Old English —

Then up from the marsh,
under misty cliffs,
Grendel came walking;
he bore God's wrath
— English translation —

LONG AGO King Hrothgar of Denmark built a towering feast hall named Herot. There each night, he hosted a sumptuous banquet and showered his guests with glittering golden treasures.

There was only one in Denmark who despised the joyous sounds that came from Herot. His name was Grendel, and he was a hideous monster who ruled the swamps and lowlands.

One dark night, during a glorious banquet, Grendel rose from his marshy lake. With gleaming yellow eyes, he prowled the misty moors until he came to King Hrothgar's great feast hall.

In the cold hour before dawn, as the king's warriors slept on the floor of Herot, Grendel crept inside. Before anyone could arm or protect himself, the monster slaughtered thirty of the king's bravest men.

At daybreak, a terrible wail rose from the hall when King Hrothgar discovered his warriors had been brutally murdered. Stunned and shaken, he grieved all that day, for he feared this horror was only the beginning.

Indeed, that very night Grendel returned to Herot, and those who could not escape him were slain.

For the next twelve years, the king's great feast hall stood empty as Grendel prowled the land. Year after year he stalked Hrothgar's warriors and seized them in the dark, murdering the defenseless men one by one.

Stories of the monster's evil acts spread far and wide. They even reached the distant shores of the Geatish nation, where a great warrior named Beowulf lived. All had heard tales of how

Beowulf had slain hideous sea monsters and an army of fierce giants.

Now Beowulf swore he would slay the monstrous enemy of King Hrothgar, and he ordered that a ship be built at once. Then he chose fifteen of the bravest warriors in his land and marched them to the shore.

With the wind behind him, Beowulf sailed his vessel over the roughest seas to the rocky shores of Denmark.

As he and his warriors climbed onto the beach, a watchman on a cliff saw their bright shields glinting in the cold light. He galloped down to the small army, waving his heavy spear at them. "Who are you?" he demanded. "Where do you come from? And why?"

"We are Geats," said Beowulf. "And I am son of Ecgtheow. We have heard that your country is cursed with a terrible monster who haunts the night. We have come to help free you from him."

The watchman led Beowulf and his warriors to the king, and the old, gray-haired man welcomed them with joy. Long ago he had been a friend of Beowulf's father.

King Hrothgar and his wife, Queen Welthrow, held a great banquet that afternoon. For the first time in twelve years, music and laughter rang out from their feast hall.

But when shadows of dark fell, the king and queen bid Beowulf good night and wished him well. All feared that the sounds of merriment and laughter had called Grendel out from his lair.

After the royal party left, Beowulf removed his iron corset and helmet. Then he put away his sword and shield. Grendel used no weapons. And Beowulf sensed that he could only defeat the monster if he fought him on his own terms.

As Beowulf and his men lay down on their bedding, none of Beowulf's young warriors expected to see morning. They knew that Grendel would soon attack.

Indeed, the creature had already risen from the marsh and had begun to walk the misty moors.

Hours later, in the gloom of the feast hall, only Beowulf was awake. He waited and listened for Grendel.

He heard the door snap apart. He heard the monster's foot-steps in the hall. He heard Grendel's cruel laughter, and he saw the yellow fire that burned in the monster's eyes.

But Beowulf pretended to sleep, for he wanted to observe the monster's method of attack.

One sleeping warrior lay between him and Grendel. Grendel seized the warrior and devoured all of him, even his hands and feet.

Then the monster lurched toward Beowulf and reached out to grab him with his bloody claws.

But Beowulf seized him, and with the strength of thirty, he gripped Grendel's arm.

For a moment, the two opponents were frozen. Grendel looked into Beowulf's ice-cold eyes and knew that Beowulf was unlike any man he'd ever known.

Grendel tried to break free, but Beowulf held him tightly. The hall shook with the sounds of their thunderous combat.

Beowulf's warriors drew their swords and slashed at Grendel, but the sharpest blade could not harm him.

Beowulf and Grendel tore the feast hall apart as they fought, until finally the sinews and tendons of the monster's shoulder cracked. Muscle slipped from the bone as Beowulf wrenched Grendel's arm free from its bloody socket.

Screaming in agony, Grendel fled out into the night. Knowing his life would soon end, he returned to his marshy lake to die.

The men's victorious cheers filled the hall as Beowulf raised Grendel's arm and clawed hand into the air.

The next day, chieftains came from far and wide and joined Beowulf and King Hrothgar's men. The warriors followed the monster's tracks to the edge of the swamp.

They rejoiced when they saw the water swirling with Grendel's blood. Then all returned to Herot to celebrate the death of the monster.

Grendel's arm swung from the rafters of the feast hall as the rowdy revelers passed cups of mead and sang songs proclaiming Beowulf a great hero.

King Hrothgar also heaped praise on Beowulf's brave acts. He gave the young warrior a victory flag, a helmet, a shimmering coat of mail, an ancient jewel-studded sword, and eight horses with golden saddles.

Queen Welthrow rewarded Beowulf with a golden-ringed collar, the greatest treasure of her people, and she wished him a long life filled with prosperity.

The guests feasted and celebrated long after dark. When Hrothgar and Welthrow had finally retired to their castle and Beowulf and his men to their special chambers, the king's warriors cleared away the banquet benches and lay down to sleep.

For the first time in twelve years, they slept soundly in the king's hall.

Little did they know, however, that while one monster had died, another still lived.

DEEP IN THE BLACK WATERS of the swamp, Grendel's mother grieved over her slain son. At midnight, she rose from the dismal marsh and began to stalk the moors.

When she entered Herot, the walls trembled with her heavy steps. This awakened the warriors, who flew for their swords and shields.

But the monster moved quickly. Leaving her muddy footprints behind, she snatched her son's arm, which was hanging from the rafters. With it, she murdered King Hrothgar's most faithful warrior; then she fled.

In the dark before dawn, Beowulf was called to Herot. There, he found the king wracked with sorrow.

"You destroyed Grendel with your death grip," Hrothgar said, "but now another has avenged his death by slaying my dearest friend."

"Grieve not," said Beowulf. "This monster, too, shall find no escape in the bowels of the earth or the bottom of the sea."

The king ordered horses for himself and Beowulf. With shield-bearing soldiers at their side, they set out for the monster's lair.

Again, a small army followed huge footprints up rocky hills, through the high wolf country, and down windy cliffs, until finally they came to the dismal, foggy marsh.

The Danes were horrified. This time, the lake was lit with strange water fires and was crawling with horrible demons. Snakes and scaly sea dragons slithered over the rocks.

Only Beowulf was not afraid. He donned his armor and helmet and his mighty sword. Then he plunged into the black pool and swam past the fires and the gruesome demons, down into the deepest waters.

For one hundred years, Grendel's mother had reigned over the muddy world at the bottom of the marsh. As soon as Beowulf entered her realm, she seized him with her long claws. She tore and scratched at his armor, but in vain. Furious, she then dragged him to her den, clutching him so tightly he could not draw his sword.

The monster's cavernous den burned with bright, hideous light. Finally, Beowulf managed to draw his sword, but when he swung it at the head of the beast, it did not harm her.

He tossed his sword aside and seized Grendel's mother by the shoulder. Anger doubled his strength, and he threw her to the muddy floor. Clouds of murky water billowed around them.

Grendel's mother slashed Beowulf with her claws. He stumbled. She pinned him down, drew her knife, and tried to stab him.

But the monster's blade was blunted by Beowulf's thick armor. Using all his might, he freed himself and struggled to his feet.

Then Beowulf spied a sword on the wall — the magic sword of the ancient giants who had ruled the world at the beginning of time. It was the mightiest weapon in the world. No human had ever lifted it.

With all his strength, Beowulf drew the giants' sword from its scabbard and held it high over his head. Then he drove the blade into the monster's body, and she fell lifeless to the floor.

When the monster's blood washed to the surface of the lake, Hrothgar and his men believed it came from Beowulf. They were certain their friend had been slain. With great sorrow, they spurred their horses and headed for home.

But Beowulf's fifteen faithful warriors stayed in the marsh, hoping desperately that their leader had survived.

As they stared at the water with heavy hearts, Beowulf burst through the surface. He emerged into the light of day, holding high the giants' magic sword.

His warriors rejoiced and gave thanks to God. They helped Beowulf onto the shore, and for the first time in one hundred years, the waters of the dismal swamp grew clear and calm.

The Danes celebrated the victory of Beowulf with a great feast. At the evening's end, King Hrothgar's men went to sleep in the golden hall of Herot without a trace of fear or foreboding.

When the bright light of morning chased away the shadows, they celebrated Beowulf's victory once more. They knew now that the great hall was truly safe.

The old king wept as he said good-bye to Beowulf. He promised that there would be peace forever between their two lands.

Bearing gifts and treasures, Beowulf and his men sailed through deep waters back to their homeland. And for the next fifty winters, Beowulf was the wise ruler of his people.

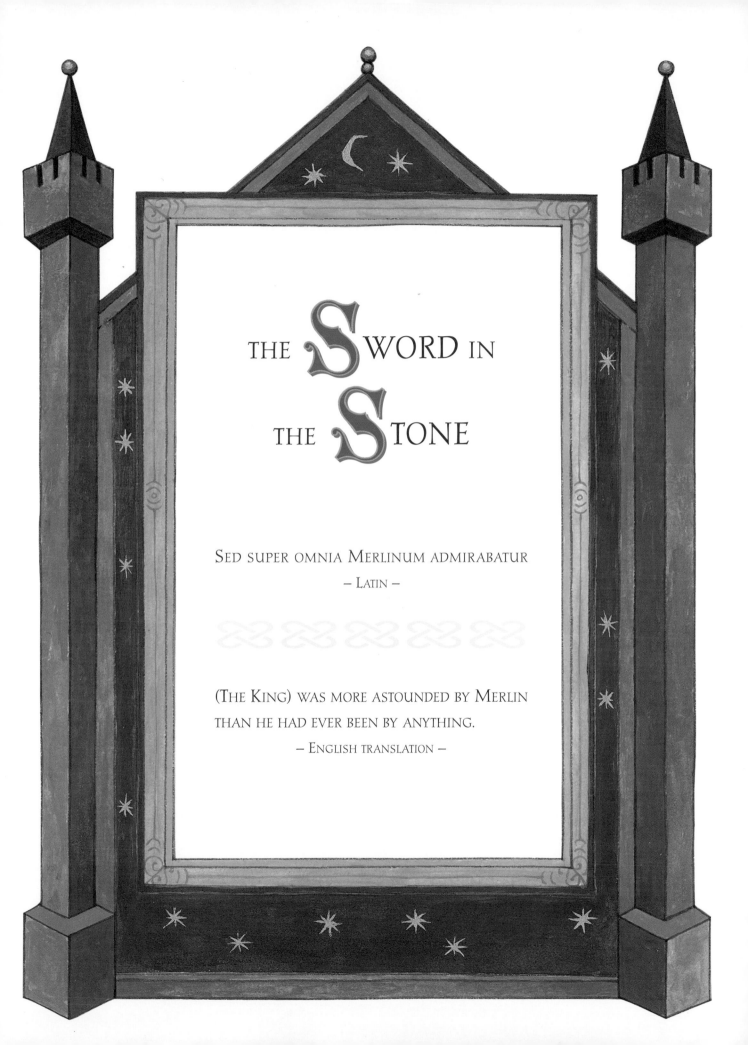

# THE SWORD IN THE STONE

Sed super omnia Merlinum admirabatur

– Latin –

(The King) was more astounded by Merlin
than he had ever been by anything.

– English translation –

Long ago in the fifth century, after the cruel Saxons had taken over half of Britain, a wicked king named Vortigern ruled the land. Three times the king tried to build a strong tower to defend his kingdom against its enemies. But each time a tower was completed, it would mysteriously topple to the ground.

Desperate to protect his kingdom, King Vortigern called his astrologers and begged for their help.

"You must mix the mortar of the tower's foundation," the astrologers advised, "with the blood of a child born without a human father."

"That's impossible," said the king. But still he ordered his men to search the land for such a child.

One day, as the king's messengers passed through a village, they came upon two boys quarreling.

"Who are *you* to compete with *me*, Merlin?" shouted one boy. "You don't count! You never even had a father!"

The messengers looked closely at the boy named Merlin, then lost no time asking the villagers about him. They soon learned that Merlin's mother was a mortal. But his father was an Incubus, a half-mortal being, invisible to the eye.

Upon the king's orders, the messengers asked the boy and his mother to come with them to the palace.

Though Merlin was only seven, he walked boldly up to the king. "Why have you sent for me?" he asked.

King Vortigern told the boy the gruesome reason.

But Merlin did not even blink. "Your astrologers are wrong," he said. "My blood will not help your tower stand. Order your men to dig in the earth beneath the foundation, and they will find a pool of water. It is this pool that makes your grounds unsteady."

The king ordered his workmen to dig into the ground; and indeed, they found the pool as Merlin had said.

"Now order your men to drain the pool," Merlin advised. "They will find two stones, and inside these hollow stones, they will find two sleeping dragons."

The astonished king did as Merlin said. His workmen drained the pool and uncovered two stones. From the stones emerged two dragons, one white and one red.

As soon as the dragons were freed, they began to fight fiercely. They breathed fire and clawed at one another, until finally, the white one killed the red one. Then it slithered away between two rocks.

Horrified, King Vortigern asked Merlin to explain what the fight of the dragons had meant.

Looking the wicked king in the eye, Merlin answered calmly. "The white dragon stands for warriors who will someday slay you," he said.

Not long afterward, all the king's men marveled over Merlin's extraordinary powers, for King Vortigern was indeed murdered by his enemies — just as the young boy had predicted.

MANY YEARS LATER, an enemy of the Saxons became the king of Britain. His name was Uther Pendragon, and Merlin was made his chief magician.

Since war still raged between the Saxons and the Britons,

Merlin used his magic gifts to predict which conflicts Uther would lose and which he would win. He drew up battle plans and brought storms and winds to help Britain's armies. He also changed into different animals or people to outwit the enemy and collect secret information.

Merlin even used his powerful magic to help Uther Pendragon win the hand of the beautiful Igraine, the woman the king desired more than any other.

When Queen Igraine and King Uther were expecting their first child, Merlin went to Uther. "Sire, you will soon have a son who is destined for glory," the enchanter said. "I wish to raise and educate him myself. Please give him to me as a reward for helping you marry your queen."

"Indeed, I will do whatever you wish," said Uther, for he was greatly in Merlin's debt.

When the king's son was born, his tearful mother wrapped the baby in a gold cloth. Then two knights and two ladies delivered the infant to Merlin, who waited at the rear of the castle dressed as a beggar.

Merlin slipped his tiny bundle away into the dark night, and the babe was not seen again.

THREE YEARS LATER, Uther Pendragon fell ill. As his sickness grew worse, Merlin went to him. "Sire, is it not your desire that your son shall someday take your place on the throne?" he asked.

The king nodded. "I bestow on my son God's blessing and my own." Then Uther Pendragon died.

For the next twelve years, the nobles of the land fought bitterly over who should ascend the throne of Britain. To protect the king's son, Merlin kept him in hiding the entire time.

Then one Christmas morning, Merlin bid the archbishop of Canterbury to gather his lords together.

When the nobles arrived, they came upon a sight they had not seen before. The night before, a mysterious stone had been set near the door of the church. And a sword had been thrust into the middle of it, with an inscription that read:

*Whosoever can pull the sword from this stone*
*is the true king of Britain.*

Two hundred and fifty nobles tried to lift the sword, but none succeeded.

The archbishop of Canterbury then chose ten men to guard the mysterious sword day and night. He proclaimed that on New Year's Day there would be a great tournament. After the tournament, all the knights in the land would gather in the churchyard and try to lift the sword from the stone.

On the day of the tournament, a young knight named Sir Kay was just about to enter the jousting competition when he discovered that his sword was missing from its sheath.

"Hurry, ride back to our lodging and find my sword!" he bid his young squire.

The squire galloped away to Sir Kay's inn. But when the boy arrived at the lodging, he found the door locked. All the inhabitants had left for the tournament.

Hating to disappoint Sir Kay, the squire decided to ride to the church. *Perhaps I can dislodge the sword from the stone and give that sword to Sir Kay,* he thought.

When the boy arrived in the churchyard, he discovered that all the guards had slipped away to the tournament. He dismounted from his horse and crept up to the sword. He grabbed it by its hilt, and with great ease he drew it out of the stone.

The squire then galloped back to the tournament and handed the sword to Sir Kay. The knight instantly recognized the prized weapon. He hid the sword under his coat, then hurried to his father, a good knight named Sir Hector.

"Father!" he cried. "I have lifted the sword that was in the stone. I am to be the next king of Britain."

Sir Hector stared thoughtfully at his son. "Come," he said. "Let's return to the churchyard, so you can show me exactly what you did."

Sir Kay and his young squire followed Sir Hector to the courtyard of the church. When they stood before the stone, Sir Hector said, "Now, demonstrate your great strength for me."

Sir Kay placed the mighty weapon back into the stone. When he tried to lift it, he failed miserably. He may as well have tried to lift the church. Ashamed, he confessed that it was, in fact, his young squire who had drawn the sword out of the stone.

"Then *you* try such a feat again," Sir Hector said to the squire.

The boy clasped the jeweled handle with both hands. Then he gracefully lifted the sword from the stone, as though he were lifting it out of clear water.

Sir Hector knelt before the young squire.

"Why are you kneeling in front of me?" the boy asked.

"My lord, only one man on Earth can draw the sword from the stone," said Sir Hector. "And he is the true king of Britain."

The boy gazed with astonishment at Sir Hector. "How is that possible?" he said.

"Fifteen years ago, Merlin the Magician carried you from the king's castle," Sir Hector began. "He had you baptized with the name Arthur, then delivered you into the care of me and my wife. We raised you as our own until you became squire to Sir Kay. But, in truth, you are the son of King Uther Pendragon. I have always known that one day you would assume your true role as king of our land."

Sir Hector delivered the news to the archbishop of Canterbury. When Arthur's kingship was announced, the jealous nobles resisted crowning the boy. But the commoners rejoiced and proclaimed Arthur their new leader.

From that time on, Arthur was king of Britain, and Merlin the Magician was his closest friend and adviser.

# Island
## of the
# Lost Children

Ez begúnde lûte erschrîen,
ez was sêre erschraht
er truog ez harte hôhe
mit der sînen maht
— Middle High German —

The boy was sorely frightened,
and began aloud to shriek;
higher the mighty griffin flew,
with outstretched beak
— English translation—

Long Ago in Holland a mighty king and queen gave birth to a remarkable son named Hagen. Even as a small boy, Prince Hagen showed great promise of courage and valor.

One summer, Hagen's father held a royal tournament. The palace and city swarmed like a beehive. In the daytime, jewels and armor glittered in the sunlight. At night in the feast halls, the sounds of harps and lutes filled the air.

On the eighth day, however, all the feasting and mirth turned to bitter sorrow. For into the midst of the sport and laughter appeared an evil griffin, a monster with the body and hind legs of a lion and the head and wings of an eagle.

The griffin lit upon a tree. Beneath it sat Prince Hagen with his nursemaid. When the maid saw the hideous creature, she ran away screaming, leaving the frightened young prince alone.

Seizing the moment, the griffin swooped down from the tree and grabbed Hagen with its claws. As it soared away, its wings roared like the wind and spread darkness over the land like a storm cloud.

The king and queen and all their guests watched in horror as the monster and Hagen vanished into the sky.

Hagen's parents nearly went mad with grief. Messengers were sent to scour the land. But they came back with neither news of the monstrous bird nor the kidnapped child. Forced to conclude that their son had been slain, the king and queen were left to their sorrow.

In truth, Hagen was not slain. The monster had already eaten that day, so his appetite did not compel him to kill the young prince. Instead, the griffin carried Hagen over land and sea until they came to a deserted island.

There, on the summit of a cliff, the griffin delivered Hagen to its nest. The monster's young began to play with the terrified boy as cats would torment a mouse. During their play, a young griffin seized Hagen and flew off with him. Hagen screamed and fought, until the griffin dropped him, and Hagen crashed to the ground.

Badly bruised and scratched, the boy dragged himself into the underbrush to hide from the flying monsters; and there he fell into a deep sleep.

The next morning Hagen awoke, feeling cold and hungry. He crept out from his shelter, hoping to find wild berries to eat.

Behind Hagen were tall pine trees; in front of him was a sandy slope stretching down to a rocky beach, where the black sea crashed with a mighty force. No roots or berries grew in that desolate place by the sea. The ground was parched and barren.

As the boy looked fearfully about, he saw three ghostlike figures moving among the pines.

Cautiously, he drew near and saw that the figures were young maidens, wearing garments woven from the gray moss that hung from the tree branches.

The eldest of the girls stepped forward bravely. "Why do you hunt us?" she asked.

"I don't," said Hagen. "I was kidnapped and brought here yesterday by a griffin."

The maiden, whose name was Hilda, was relieved to discover that Hagen was not a wild creature, but a mere child like herself.

She saw that he was bruised and battered from his terrible journey. So she led him to the cave where she and the other two young girls were hiding from the griffins.

In the cave, the three maidens made Hagen lie down on a bed of moss. They washed dirt and blood from his hands and face and gave him water to drink.

When Hagen asked them for food, they shared the herbs they had gathered at daybreak before the griffins had stirred.

After he had eaten, Hagen told the girls his name and how he had arrived at the island.

Each maiden then explained how she, too, had been kidnapped by the griffin and how she had escaped the monster's claws and found the others. For three years now the maidens had lived together in their cave, safe from the griffins and other wild creatures of the wood.

The eldest of them, Hilda, was the daughter of a king in India; the next oldest came from Sweden; and the youngest came from Portugal. All three loved Hagen and gave him food and water each day to help him recover from his terrible ordeal.

With no hope for escape, Hagen and the three maidens lived together on the lonely island for four summers and four winters. They never ventured beyond the edge of the wood for fear of the griffins.

One night, a terrible storm hit the island. Lightning struck the pines. The sea roared and lashed the shore. The children huddled together as salt water gusted into the opening of their cave.

When morning dawned, Hagen looked out at the sea and saw a deserted ship rolling on the waves.

For a better view, he snuck down to the edge of the shore; and to his horror, he saw the drowned bodies of sailors sprawled across the rocks. The accident had attracted the hideous griffins, who were fighting over the corpses.

Hagen fled back to the cave and told his friends what he had seen. They all wept for the fate of the brave men who had died at sea.

The next morning Hagen rose early again and slipped back down to the water in search of any goods that might have washed ashore.

He found the rocks strewn with planks and chests from the ship. When he saw a drowned sailor clad in shining armor, he took the armor for his own. He buckled it around his body, then strapped on the warrior's sword and bow.

As Hagen started back to the cave, he felt a rush of wind and heard a screeching cry. Then he saw a huge griffin flying toward him.

Unable to escape, Hagen flashed his sword at the monster. The griffin attacked with its beak and tried to peck out his eyes, but Hagen sliced the air with his sword and cut the monster's wing. With another stab, he slashed the griffin's leg, and the creature fell to the ground.

The other griffins swooped down on Hagen. From their cave, the maidens watched in horror as the boy defended himself. He swung his mighty sword, killing one flying monster after another.

Finally, after the last griffin had fallen to the rocks, Hagen ran toward the cave. "Come out!" he shouted joyfully. "Feel the air and the sun! We're free!"

The maidens rushed forward and praised Hagen for his great strength and courage.

After much rejoicing, the lost children started across the deserted island, in search of a smooth shore where a ship might be able to land. They walked day and night, guiding themselves by the sun and the stars.

With his sword and bow, Hagen fought off all the wild beasts. He was king of the woods — leaping like a panther and fighting like a lion. Together, he and the maidens hunted and fished. They gathered wood and made fires and feasted on wild boar and venison.

One day, they finally came to a sandy shore. Miraculously, a ship was sailing by. The lost children shouted and jumped up and down.

The vessel started in their direction. But as it came closer, the sailors saw the maidens in their strange mossy garments and mistook them for sea monsters.

The ship started to move away. But Hagen jumped on a rock and shouted for help. The sailors heard his words and realized that these were indeed humans. They turned around and hurried toward shore with great speed.

The owner of the ship, the Count of Garadie, invited the four children to come aboard, and he fed them a great feast.

At the table, Hagen explained how they had been carried off by griffins and how he had slain the monsters.

The count stared at him in astonishment, for all knew that one griffin was a match for five strong men.

"Tell me," he said to the boy, "who is your father?"

"He is King Sigeband," answered Hagen.

The count smiled grimly. "Ah, it is well that you have fallen into my hands. I will now avenge myself on your father. He drove me from my castle and slew all my knights. I will hold you prisoner for his wicked deeds."

Hagen held up his sword and stared coldly at the count. "I will not be your hostage," the boy said. "If my father has done wrong, take us to him, and I promise he will repay you a thousandfold."

The count ordered his crew to sail at once to the harbor of Balyan, the home of King Sigeband.

"Go to my mother," Hagen told the count's messengers. "Tell her that you know where her son is. If she doubts you, tell her that her son has a little cross the color of gold marked on his chest. By that sign she will know you are telling the truth."

The messengers rode to the castle and were taken before the king.

When Sigeband heard they were from Garadie, he stiffened with anger. "How dare you enter here!" he said. "You know I have sworn to hang all of the people of Garadie."

"But your son Hagen has sent us," said a messenger. "We rescued him at sea."

"How wicked your lies are," said Sigeband. "My son Hagen died four years ago. We weep for him every day."

"Well, he who calls himself Prince Hagen bears the mark of the cross upon his chest, a gold cross," said the messenger. "He told us that his mother will know him by this sign."

The queen gasped. "Let us ride down to the harbor," she said. "And we can see for ourselves whether or not our son has returned."

The king and queen mounted horses, and, with their chief knights and ladies, they rode down to the harbor of Balyan.

When Hagen saw the party approaching, he came ashore to greet them.

The queen bade the crowd to clear a space. Then she asked Hagen to uncover his chest. There, for certain, was the mark of the gold cross.

The queen cried out with inexpressible joy and embraced her long-lost son.

No less was the joy of the king, who wept aloud before all his people. To the Count of Garadie, he promised peace forever more. And for the next fourteen days, he hosted a great feast for Hagen, the three maidens, the count, and all the court.

The whole land rejoiced. Soon thereafter, Sigeband bestowed his crown upon Hagen. And the young king asked the maiden Hilda to be his wife and his queen. Together, they ruled wisely for many years.

# THE SONG
## OF ROLAND

ROLLANS AD MIS L'OLIFAN À SA BUCHE,
EMPEINT-LE BEN, PAR GRANT VERTUT LE SUNET.
— OLD FRENCH —

ROLAND HAS SET THE HORN TO HIS MOUTH,
HE GRASPS IT WELL
AND WITH GREAT VIRTUE SOUNDS.
— ENGLISH TRANSLATION —

CHARLEMAGNE, the mighty king of France, had been at war with Spain for seven long years. In the name of Christianity, he had conquered the country as far as the sea. No castle or rampart was left to be destroyed. Only the city of Saragossa high upon a mountain remained.

One day, the pagan king of Spain summoned his dukes and counts to his court in Saragossa. "Lord Barons," he said, "Charlemagne will soon try to destroy us. I have no army to match his. Give me advice as to how we can avoid more shame and death."

The king's wisest knight stepped forward. "Offer Charlemagne an olive branch as a symbol of your service and friendship, sire. And give him hundreds and thousands of gifts."

"And what if Charlemagne still does not believe in our good will?" asked the king of Spain.

"We will send him our own sons as hostages — even if it means their death. Better they should lose their heads than we should lose all the beautiful land of Spain."

The king decided to follow the counsel of his wisest knight, so he sent ten horsemen to meet with Charlemagne.

The Spanish emissaries found the French king in his garden with his warriors. The Franks were all quite happy, for they had just shattered the walls of Cordoba, captured the city, and taken all its gold and silver.

As his men played chess and practiced their fencing beneath the pine trees, the white-bearded Charlemagne sat with them in his golden chair. The king's noble stature and his fierce expression left no doubt as to which of them was the leader of all France.

As soon as the emissaries had given their message to Charlemagne, the king summoned his nobles to him. Among them was the bravest and most beloved of his warriors — his nephew, Count Roland.

When Roland heard of the pagan offering, he grew very angry. "If you believe the good will of the king of Spain, you will regret it," he said. "Once before he offered you the olive branch of peace, and later he betrayed you and cut off the heads of your men. Lay siege to his city at once, and avenge those whom he put to death!"

Ganelon, Roland's wicked stepfather, scoffed at these words. "Trust the speech of Count Roland, and you will regret it," he said. "We should make peace with the king of Spain."

"Then perhaps someone should journey to the pagan fortress," said Charlemagne, "and find out what lies behind this peace offering."

"Send Ganelon," said Roland, "since he is so certain of the good will of Spain."

Ganelon glared at Roland. His jealousy of his stepson made him despise the youth. Furthermore, he resented the suggestion that he undertake such a dangerous mission, for he lacked true courage and strength.

But Charlemagne thought Roland's idea an excellent one. "Yes, of course!" he said. "Ganelon must leave at once."

Furious, Ganelon set out for the pagan fortress, vowing to take revenge on Roland. By the time he arrived at the king of

Spain's castle, he was more an enemy of the Franks than an enemy of the pagans.

As soon as he greeted the king, Ganelon began to plot with him. "Give your gifts to Charlemagne," he said, "let him start for France. When his army gets to the mountains, order your men to attack. I'll make certain that Count Roland is captain of the rear guard so he can quickly be slain. His death will break the spirit of Charlemagne, for he is the king's right arm. The Franks will fight you no more, and you can live in peace."

The enemy thanked Ganelon for his act of treason and gave him many gifts. Then the traitor returned to Charlemagne and urged him to trust the pagans. "The king of Spain will become your vassal," he promised.

Charlemagne praised Ganelon's success, then ordered the Franks to break camp and start at once for home. As he had promised the pagans, Ganelon had Roland appointed captain of the rear guard.

On a clear, sunlit day, Roland and his closest friend, Count Oliver, led twenty thousand soldiers through the Valley of Thorns in the Pyrenees mountains.

Suddenly, they heard the distant sound of trumpets.

Oliver climbed a hill. When he looked south, he saw crimson, blue, and white banners floating above a sea of glittering helmets and shields. At least four hundred thousand pagan soldiers were marching after them. At least a thousand were blowing trumpets.

"Roland, we're going to be attacked!" cried Oliver. "Blow your horn so Charlemagne will hear and come back!"

ROLAND BLEW  WITH ALL HIS MIGHT

"No, I will not sound my horn and endanger the king's entire army," said Roland. "We must fight them ourselves."

Count Roland stood on a hill and called to his men: "A battle draws near! Dismount and pray! Then strike a blow for God!"

As Roland rode his swift horse down the ranks of his twenty thousand men, the white pennants of his lance streamed behind him, and the battle cry "Mountjoy!" rang through the air.

When the pagans attacked, Roland became fiercer than a lion. He spurred his horse and rode into battle. He struck fifteen mighty blows with his lance until it was in shards. Then he drew his sword and wreaked havoc against the enemy. Though the pagans threw spears, lances, and feathered javelins at him, he kept fighting.

On four assaults, the Franks killed thousands of pagans. But on the fifth, the tide turned, and almost all the French knights were slain. As they died, a terrible storm hit their country. Thunder, lightning, winds, and earthquakes shook the land.

At noon a great darkness covered all of France. The Franks believed the world was about to end. In truth, it was nature grieving for the impending death of Count Roland.

With his friends lying dead, the brave warrior decided to blow his horn. This way, Charlemagne's men would know to come and bear away the bodies of their comrades rather than leave them to the wolves.

Roland blew his horn with all his might. He blew so hard that his temples burst. Blood streamed from his ears and mouth, but still he kept blowing his horn.

King Charlemagne halted when he heard the distant sound. He turned his men around, and they answered Roland's call with sixty thousand bugles. The mountains rang with the deafening sound.

Hearing this, Roland put down his horn and returned to battle with a vengeance. Though Roland was wounded, the enemy took flight from him like deer running from a pack of hounds.

Roland struck one, then another, until even the king of Spain and a hundred thousand pagan soldiers fled in fear.

Roland picked up his horn and blew again, but this time, the sound grew faint. In the far distance, Charlemagne was seized by a terrible grief, for he knew his beloved nephew was dying.

But Roland, a man of uncommon strength, could not be vanquished like any mortal. He remained on his feet and wandered the battlefield, searching for his dead friends. He carried them, one after the other, to the wounded archbishop to be blessed.

Finally, Roland picked up the body of his dearest friend, Oliver. Weeping, Roland spoke soft words to Oliver as he carried his body to the archbishop. After he laid his friend on the earth, Roland could bear his pain no longer. The color drained from his face, and he sank to the ground.

But the warrior roused himself one last time and rose and staggered across the battlefield. When he fell again, he lay still, and memories of his homeland surged through his mind — memories of the battles he had fought and the people he had loved.

Roland raised his right glove to Heaven. As if in a dream, he saw Saint Gabriel take it from him. Then Count Roland dropped his weary head and died.

When Charlemagne arrived at the scene, he hopelessly wandered the battlefield, stepping between slain warriors, shouting, "Roland! Oliver!"

The king called for the archbishop, too. But only the screams of circling vultures answered his cries.

When the bodies of his favorite warriors were finally discovered, Charlemagne and his knights raged with grief.

The king vowed to avenge their sorrow. He prayed to God to extend the sunlight far into the night, so his army could stop the pagans once and for all.

The sunlight remained to the battle's end as the Franks defeated their enemy. Afterward, warriors and horses slept throughout the grassy meadows.

Only Charlemagne stayed awake beneath the full moon. Still dressed in his shining armor, the king sat and rested for the first time all day.

"Dear Roland, my friend," he whispered, "when I return to France, all who love you will ask of you. And I will tell them that you stood and fought bravely to the end, until God sent his angels to carry your soul to paradise."

Then Charlemagne bowed his head and wept.

# THE WEREWOLF

QUANT DES LAIS FAIRE M'ENTREMET,
NE VOIL UBLIER BISCLAVRET
— OLD FRENCH —

AMONGST THE TALES I TELL YOU ONCE AGAIN,
I WOULD NOT FORGET
THE LAY OF THE WERE-WOLF.
— ENGLISH TRANSLATION —

LONG AGO in northern France, a valiant knight named Sir Marrok was married to a fair lady who loved him tenderly. One thing, however, made the lady unhappy with her husband: Every week, he disappeared for three days, and no one knew where he went.

The lady grew more and more troubled by her husband's disappearances, until finally she could bear it no longer. One day after Sir Marrok had returned from one of his mysterious trips, she approached him. "My dear lord," she said, "I must ask you something, but I'm afraid my question will make you angry."

Sir Marrok embraced his wife. "Fear not," he said. "I will tell you anything within my power to tell."

"I am very frightened when you leave me alone," she said. "I dread losing you, for I do not know where you go. Pray, tell me, what is your secret?"

The knight looked pained. "Please ask me no more questions. If I told you the truth, only evil would come of it. You would begin to loathe me, and I would be lost."

But his wife persisted. "I could never loathe you," she said. "Please tell me, where do you go?"

Day and night, the wife wept and begged her husband to tell her where he went, until finally, he was forced to share his terrible secret.

"Long ago an evil spell was cast upon me," he said. "Each week, I become a werewolf. As soon as I feel the change coming on, I hide in the thickest part of the forest. I live there, hunting and eating wild roots for three days and three nights. Then I change back into a human."

The man's wife was so repelled she could barely speak. "But what of your garments?" she stammered. "Do you still wear them when you are a wolf?"

"I lay my clothing aside," said Sir Marrok. "That's all I can say. I cannot tell you more because if I were to lose my garments, I would remain a wolf for all time."

"Oh, please tell me, my lord," the lady said. "Why do you hide this last thing? Surely you do not think that the one who loves you most would betray you."

Sir Marrok sighed. "At the edge of the forest is an old chapel. Near the chapel is a large stone with a hollow beneath it. I hide my garments in the hollow. When the enchantment loses its power, I put them back on and return home."

After the lady heard her husband's story, her love for him changed. Just as Sir Marrok had feared, she was seized with great loathing for him. Night and day she dreamed of how she might escape his embrace.

Finally, the lady sent for a certain knight who had once loved her and tried to woo her. She swore him to secrecy, then told him the story about her husband.

The knight was horrified, and he asked how he could help her.

"You must steal his clothes," the lady said. "Then my husband will not be able to change back into a man, and he'll be forced to live as a wolf in the forest for all his days, until someone finally slays him."

Soon after, the lady's friend went forth and stole Sir Marrok's garments from under the large stone near the chapel. When he brought them to her, she hid them well. "Now I am safe!" she exclaimed. "That beast will never return to my home."

Time passed, and when Sir Marrok did not return, his wife pretended to worry about him. She even sent men to look for him. But they found no trace of him, and all concluded that he had been mysteriously slain on one of his secret journeys.

After a year had passed, the lady wed the knight who had helped her. They took over all of Sir Marrok's lands and possessions, and neither worried anymore about the good man they had betrayed.

MEANWHILE, THE POOR WOLF roamed the forest, grieving bitterly for the wife he had loved so well.

One day he heard the barking of the king's hounds. He knew the dogs had caught his scent and would soon be upon him. He bounded through the woods, but the dogs chased after him.

All day, the wolf fled the hounds, until at last they closed in on him. Just as he was about to be overtaken and torn to pieces, the king caught up to his dogs.

The wolf dashed to the king and seized him by the boot. He licked it as if begging for mercy.

The king stared at the wolf in astonishment. "Look here, my lords!" he called. "What is this marvel? A wolf asking me for my help! Why, the beast acts like a man. Call off the dogs. I do not want this creature injured. I order no one should hunt in this forest, lest by accident they slay this remarkable animal."

But when the king and his men started for home, the wolf did not linger in the forest. Rather, he followed close behind the royal party. He would not turn back, not even when they arrived at the king's castle.

The king was greatly pleased, for he thought the wolf quite wondrous. He ordered his knights to treat the beast with great care and kindness. And he allowed the wolf to sleep in his own chamber.

As the wolf roamed freely about the court, all the courtiers were very impressed with him, for he moved about with such grace and intelligence that he seemed almost human.

One day the king called his knights and barons together for an annual meeting. Among the nobles was the knight who had betrayed Sir Marrok and married his wife. The knight had no idea that his rival was still alive, much less that he was close by. But as soon as he looked upon the wolf, the animal sprang at him savagely.

The wolf would have slain the knight, had not the king called him off.

Everyone was astonished, for the wolf had never tried to hurt a soul. Someone had to guard the wolf the entire time the king held court. Not until the barons left the castle did the wolf return to his gentle self.

That spring, the king decided to journey to the forest where he had first found the wolf. As was his custom, he took the beast with him.

When Sir Marrok's wife heard that the king would soon be in her part of the country, she grew very excited. She hoped to win his favor by presenting him with splendid gifts, for she knew the king did not love her second husband as much as he had loved Sir Marrok.

But as soon as the lady entered the king's presence, the wolf attacked her and bit off her nose.

The king's men drew their swords. They would have slain the beast, if a wise courtier had not stopped them.

"Sire, this wolf has been with us a long time. He has never shown ill will to anyone except this woman and her husband. We know she was once married to a man who vanished. Heed my words — put these two in prison. Ask them if they can give a reason why the wolf should hate them so."

The king did as the wise man recommended. Before her inquisitors, the lady confessed that she had betrayed her first husband by stealing his garments. The king commanded his guards to fetch the clothes belonging to the lost Sir Marrok.

When they were brought forward, however, the wolf acted completely unconcerned.

"Sire," said the wise courtier, "if this beast is indeed a werewolf, he will not change shape while any of us watch. Leave him and the garments alone in your chambers. And we shall see if he becomes a man."

So the beast was locked in the king's private chamber. And the king and his courtiers waited for a long time before unlocking the doors.

Once they did, they found the long-lost Sir Marrok asleep on the king's couch.

The king ran to him and embraced him, and he bid Sir Marrok to take back all his stolen possessions.

The treacherous wife and her second husband were banished from the king's country. Thereafter, they lived many years in a strange land. They had children and grandchildren — but by this sign, their treachery was always known: All the maidens in the family were born without noses.

# Sir Gawain
## and the
# Green Knight

WEL GAY WATZ THIS GOME      GERED IN GRENE
& THE HERE OF HIS HED      OF HIS HORS SWETE
– MIDDLE ENGLISH –

GARBED ALL IN GREEN
WAS THE GALLANT RIDER
AND THE HAIR OF HIS HEAD
WAS THE SAME GREEN AS HIS HORSE.
– ENGLISH TRANSLATION –

EVERY WINTER, during the Yuletide festival, King Arthur and his Knights of the Round Table gathered in a great hall to feast, sing, and tell the most wondrous tales. One year, scarcely had their feast begun, when the oddest-looking man anyone had ever seen entered the hall on horseback.

The horseman was the tallest knight in the land. He was very handsome with gigantic limbs, a thick, broad chest, and a beard as big as a bush. He might have been the most handsome horse-man on Earth, but for one thing: He was green. From head to foot, his skin, hair, beard, and clothing were as green as emerald stones. His bridle was green, his saddle was green, and his horse was green. He wore no armor and carried no spear or shield. In one hand, he held a green holly bough and in the other, a great green axe.

"Who is the leader of this feast?" he bellowed.

The banquet guests could not even speak. Only King Arthur had the courage to answer the Green Knight. "Dismount from your horse, sir!" he commanded, "and join our celebration."

"I came not to feast," said the Green Knight, "but to prove the courage of your famous warriors."

"Oh, if you seek a battle, there are many here who will take you up on your offer," said the king.

The Green Knight laughed loudly. "I've not come to fight with beardless children," he shouted. "I came to play a sport. I challenge any of you to strike me with my own axe — on the condition that should I survive, next year at this time, I shall strike you back."

"Give me your axe," said King Arthur, "and I shall grant your wish."

The Green Knight dismounted from his horse. As he put his axe in the king's hands, the Knights of the Round Table shouted their protests.

"This is not a task for our king!" said Sir Gawain, the youngest of all. "Let this fight be mine."

"So be it," said King Arthur. As he gave the axe to Sir Gawain, he whispered, "Put such heart and hand in your stroke that he will never be able to pay you back."

The Green Knight grinned at the young warrior. "First, on your honor, you must swear to seek me out in twelve months and let me give back what I receive from you," the giant said.

"I swear it, on my honor," said Sir Gawain.

The Green Knight then bared his neck and waited to receive his due.

Sir Gawain swung the heavy axe with all his strength, and with one mighty blow, the sharp blade cut off the knight's head.

But the green giant did not die. He did not even flinch. Calmly and slowly, he stood up, picked up his own head, and held it aloft like a lantern. Then he mounted his horse and rode out of the hall.

The guests were stunned. Before the Green Knight had passed from sight, the severed head called out to Sir Gawain, "Remember — in a year's time, we meet again! You will find me on the day of New Year at the Green Chapel. Do not fail to keep your promise, or you will be dishonored!"

Even the bravest warrior shuddered. Preserving a knight's

honor was more important than preserving his own life. All knew that in a year's time, the Green Knight would cut off Sir Gawain's head.

Over the next months, the young knight dreaded the passing of each day. He watched winter turn to spring and spring to fall. On the Eve of All Hallows, he knew it was time to begin his long journey.

Sir Gawain bid farewell to his friends and kinsmen. Then, wearing full armor, he left Camelot and began to wander far and wide in search of the Green Knight.

Sir Gawain climbed many hills and crossed many rivers; he valiantly escaped dangerous wild beasts and savage men. In the winter cold, he slept on naked rocks and endured sleet and snow.

On Christmas Eve, Sir Gawain found himself lost in a great forest. No paths could be seen; no voices heard. He prayed for help. Then, as he raised his eyes, he saw for the first time an opening between the trees. Through the opening, he spied a castle on a distant hilltop, shining in the glow of the waning winter light.

Sir Gawain reached the castle before nightfall.

The drawbridge was lowered, and the guards of the castle announced to their lord that a wayfarer had arrived.

A tall, sturdy knight and his fair lady came out to greet Sir Gawain. They convinced the youth that he could not spend Christmas alone with the bears and the wolves, but must join them for their holiday celebration.

For three days, Sir Gawain stayed in the wonderful castle. As the day of the New Year drew nigh, he told his hosts that he must leave soon, for he was bound by his honor to find the Green Knight.

"Oh, please stay just three more days," his host urged him, "for the Green Chapel of the Green Knight is not far from here."

Surprised to discover that his journey was nearly over, Sir Gawain agreed to stay for three more days.

"Wonderful!" said his host. "Now, you must rest here at the castle while I go out to hunt. And let us have an agreement — whatever you get each day shall be mine in exchange for what I win in the woods."

Sir Gawain did not fully understand this agreement, but with good faith, he went along with it.

The next day, the lord of the castle left before daybreak with his huntsmen and hounds, while Sir Gawain rested in his chambers.

Soon the fair lady of the castle entered Sir Gawain's room. She confessed that she had fallen in love with him, and she begged him to take her away.

Sir Gawain was tempted to do as she asked, for indeed, she was very beautiful, and her words of flattery touched his heart. But the knight's sense of honor forbade him to betray his host. So he told the fair lady he could not do as she asked.

The lady only laughed merrily, and on her way out of his room, she gave him a quick kiss.

That night, the lord of the castle returned with a deer and gave it to Sir Gawain. According to their agreement, the young knight was supposed to turn over whatever he himself had gotten that day, so he gave the lord the quick kiss given him by the fair lady.

The next morning, the lord set out to hunt again. And, again, in his absence, his wife visited Sir Gawain and begged him to take her away with him. Again the young knight fought hard against the temptation to do as she asked; and again, his honor prevailed. The fair lady only laughed merrily, then gave him two quick kisses as she left.

That night, the lord returned with a boar. And he gave it to Sir Gawain in exchange for the two quick kisses the knight had received that day.

The third day was cold and clear. Once more, the lord went hunting. And once more, his wife tried to tempt their guest, but failed. This time before leaving his chambers, she gave Sir Gawain a green silk belt fringed with gold.

"Know that whoever wears this belt has the power to make any weapon harmless," she said.

Sir Gawain did not want to take her gift as he did not think it honorable. But he was overwhelmed by the fear of losing his head to the Green Knight. So he accepted the magic belt in hopes that it would save his life.

Later that day, the castle lord brought home the skin of an old fox and gave it to the young knight. But this time Sir Gawain did not keep his part of their agreement. He kept his green belt concealed and did not offer it to the lord of the castle.

That night, Sir Gawain slept poorly, for the next day was the day he had been dreading. Before the cock crowed, bringing in a stormy New Year's Day, he rose and carefully wrapped the green belt around his waist. Then he mounted his horse and set out to find the Green Knight through the wind and snow.

A servant led Sir Gawain toward the Green Chapel of the Green Knight. In the early, gray twilight, the two climbed rugged cliffs and crossed dark moors. As the sun rose, the servant prepared to leave Sir Gawain at the mouth of a valley winding between snowcapped hills.

"If you are ready to be done with life," the servant said, "then ride down to the bottom of the valley, for there is the man you seek. For all the gold on Earth, I would not go with you."

The servant turned back, leaving Sir Gawain to ride on alone.

The valley was bordered by steep stone cliffs. Look as he might, Sir Gawain did not see a chapel. He saw only the opening of a distant, dark cave.

He tied his horse to a tree and climbed the snowy rocks until he reached the mouth of the cave. "Who dwells here?" he shouted.

"Stand still!" replied a deep voice above him. "Receive now what you have come for!"

A giant figure emerged from behind the rocks, bearing a mighty axe. It was the Green Knight, his head attached again to his shoulders.

"Put down your spear!" the Green Knight said. "Take off your helmet. Stand the blow I have owed you for these twelve months."

Sir Gawain sighed. "I am ready," he said. Then he unlaced his helmet and leaned forward without fear, offering his bare neck to the steel blade.

The Green Knight raised his green axe high, then swung it through the air.

Sir Gawain did not move as the sharp edge of the axe touched his neck. It gently pierced his skin, causing only a few drops of blood to sprinkle on the snow. And that was all.

Stunned, Sir Gawain felt for his head — *it was still there*. He drew his sword and faced the knight. "One stroke have I taken," he said, "and that is all I will take — according to our agreement!"

The Green Knight turned toward him. His face was no longer green; in fact, it was the face of the lord of the castle Sir Gawain had visited.

"Brave knight, be not angry," said the lord. "I had instructed my wife to tempt you, but you passed the test of faith and honor that every true knight must pass."

Sir Gawain was confused by the generosity of the castle lord. "Cursed be my cowardice, for indeed I *was* false to my word," he said. "I kept this green belt from you." He unclasped the belt and held it out to his host.

"Nay, you must keep it," said the castle lord. "I know already of this deceit and have punished you for it, by slightly piercing your neck. You must keep it forever to remind yourself of your adventure with the Green Knight."

Sir Gawain hung his head sadly. "Ah, but this belt shall always remind me that I failed through cowardice," he said.

"Nay, not cowardice," the lord said gently. "Let it remind you instead that you love life very much. It was this very love that caused you to conceal the green belt from me, so that you might live."

The lord then invited Sir Gawain back to his castle. But the young knight was eager to return home. He said good-bye, and homeward he rode.

Many days later, all of Camelot welcomed Sir Gawain with great joy, as if he had just returned from the dead.

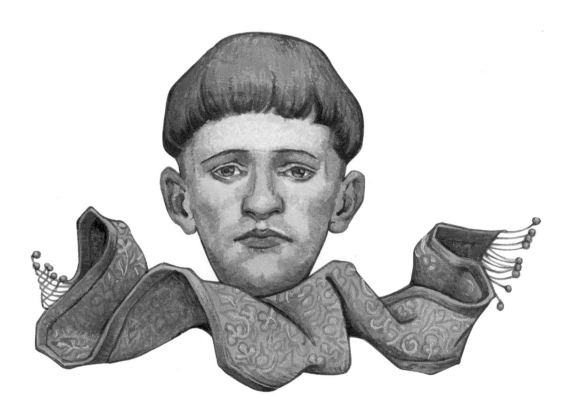

# Robin Hood
## AND HIS
# Merry Men

Lythe and listin, gentilmen,
That be of frebore blode.
I shale you tel of a gode yeman,
His name was Robyn Hode.
– Middle English –

Give ear and listen, gentlemen,
Who are of freeborn blood.
I shall tell you of a good yeoman,
His name was Robin Hood.
– English translation –

ONE DAY, long ago, King Henry of England summoned the sheriff of Nottingham to his court.

"I hear a bold outlaw named Robin Hood hides in Sherwood Forest," the king said. "The knave and his band of merry men make a sport of robbing my wealthy subjects, and then giving their booty to the poor. What have you done about him?"

The sheriff knelt humbly before the king. "My Lord and Sovereign," he said, "I have sent messengers to Sherwood Forest to arrest Robin Hood. But he beats them all and steals their warrants."

"Fie! You must do what you can to enforce my laws!" the king roared. "Devise some plan to capture Robin Hood — or else!"

The sheriff was furious as he rode away from the king's castle. "Somehow I must trick Robin Hood into coming to Nottingham Town," he growled to his man-at-arms. "Then I can lay my own hands on him!"

All the way home, the sheriff turned the matter over, until at last he slyly stroked his beard. "I have it," he said. "I will have an archery contest and offer a grand prize. Robin Hood has enough conceit to imagine he might win — and hence, he will come out of hiding."

The sheriff sent his messengers to towns and hamlets throughout the countryside to announce an archery contest that would soon take place in Nottingham Town. The winner would receive an arrow made of the purest gold.

When Robin Hood heard the news, he gathered his men under the greenwood tree. "One of us can surely win the golden arrow," he said. "Let's take our bows and arrows and go to town. What say you, lads?"

"Wait!" said the youngest member of the band. "I come straight from the Blue Boar where I heard news of the match. The sheriff's own man-at-arms confided to me that he is laying a trap for an outlaw. We must stay in the forest lest we all meet with woe."

"Thank you, lad," said Robin. "But never let it be said that the sheriff of Nottingham can frighten Robin Hood and his men. Clothe yourselves as friars, peasants, tinkers, and beggars! Carry a good bow or broadsword. As for myself, if I win the golden arrow, I'll hang it high from this greenwood tree!"

On the day of the match, the archery range of Nottingham Town was bedecked with ribbons and garlands of flowers. At one end stood the target; and at the other, all the archers gathered in a tent of striped canvas.

Around the range were seats filled with wealthy nobles, who arrived in carts or upon gaily decorated palfreys. The poorer folk sat upon the grass and dirt.

Soon the sheriff entered upon his milk white horse. He wore a purple velvet cap, a robe trimmed with ermine, and a golden chain that hung about his neck.

When he was seated, the herald sounded three blasts on a silver horn, and the archers stepped up to their marks.

The herald announced the rules of the game: "Each man will

shoot an arrow. Then the ten who shoot best will compete again. Three finalists will go against one another."

The sheriff leaned forward, keeping an eye out for Robin Hood. But not one of the archers was clad in Lincoln green, the only color ever worn by the outlaw.

"I see him not in the huge crowd," the sheriff said, "but surely he'll end up being one of the ten best. Then I will catch him."

Each archer took a turn, until ten finalists were left to compete with one another. At least six of the ten were famous for their skills. Two others were from Yorkshire, another from London Town, and the last was a beggar who was dressed in scarlet rags and wore a patch over one eye.

"Look carefully," the sheriff said to his man-at-arms. "Do you see Robin Hood among them?"

"Nay, your worship," answered the other. "Six of the men we all know well. Of the Yorkshire men, one is too tall and the other too short. The fellow from London Town has shoulders that are not nearly as broad as Robin's. And as for the beggar in the scarlet, he has a brown beard while Robin Hood has a golden one. Furthermore, he is blind in one eye and Robin is not."

"Ah," said the sheriff, "so now we have learned that Robin Hood is a coward as well as a knave. He stayed hidden in the forest today, afraid to show his face among good men."

As the first nine archers took their turns, they received roars of approval, for each had friends and supporters among the throng.

But when the beggar in scarlet rags stepped forward, not one cheer from the crowd greeted him.

The beggar drew his bow and let an arrow fly so swiftly that it could scarcely be seen. The arrow landed very close to the center of the target.

Thus, the beggar was chosen with two others to compete one last time. The audience cheered for two of the contestants, but not for the beggar. However, when the ragged stranger let his arrow fly, it sailed through the sunlit air and landed in the very center of the target.

The crowd watched with amazement as the sheriff hurried down to the stranger who had won the contest.

"Congratulations, good fellow!" he said, handing the beggar the golden arrow. "Take your prize and tell us your name."

"Some call me Jock O'Teviotdale," said the beggar.

"Well, Jock, you are the best archer in the land," said the sheriff. "I trust you draw a better bow than that cowardly outlaw Robin Hood, who dared not show his face here today."

"Ah, is that so?" said the beggar.

"Yes, and I invite you to join my service to help me fight the knave," said the sheriff. "I will give you a good coat and guarantee you decent food and ale. Surely such a life is better than the one you lead now."

"Not so, sir," said the stranger. "And I must refuse your generous offer, as no man in all England shall ever be my master."

The beggar's words angered the proud sheriff. "Then leave my town at once!" he hissed. "Before I am tempted to punish you for your insolence."

LATER THAT DAY, a motley band of outlaws gathered in Sherwood Forest, some dressed as barefoot friars, some as tinkers, some as peasants. In the middle of the group, a man hung a golden arrow from the greenwood tree.

When his job was done, he pulled a black patch from his eye and took off the scarlet rags that hid his green garments beneath. "These come off easily enough," he said. "I only wish the walnut stain would disappear as quickly from my beard!"

The outlaws laughed loudly and toasted Robin Hood for his great victory of the day. While the band feasted and quaffed ale, Robin took his best friend, Little John, aside. "It vexes me that the Sheriff of Nottingham should think I am a coward," he said. "Let us send him a message with news he does not expect."

Later that day, as the sheriff dined in his great hall, he talked with his men about the archery contest. "By my troth," he said, "I thought for certain that knave Robin Hood would be at the game today. But . . ."

Before he could finish, something flew through the window and landed on his plate. It was a blunted gray goose arrow with a fine scroll tied near its head. One of the men-at-arms picked it up and handed it to the sheriff.

The sheriff opened the scroll. Then his cheeks flushed with anger as he read:

*Now Heaven bless thy grace this day,*
*Say all in Sweet Sherwood,*
*For thou did give the prize away*
*To merry Robin Hood!*

# CHANTICLEER
## AND THE
# FOX

THIS CHAUNTECLEER STOOD HYE UP-ON HIS TOOS,
STRECCHING HIS NEKKE, AND HEELD HIS EYEN CLOOS,
AND GAN TO CROWE LOUDE FOR THE NONES
AS DAUN RUSSEL THE FOX STERTE UP AT ONES
– MIDDLE ENGLISH –

THIS CHANTICLEER STOOD HIGH UPON HIS TOES,
STRETCHING HIS NECK AND HELD HIS EYES CLOSED
AND BEGAN TO CROW LOUDLY ALL AT ONCE
AND SIR RUSSEL THE FOX LEAPED UP AT ONCE
– ENGLISH TRANSLATION –

ONCE UPON A TIME, a poor old widow lived in a small cottage near the woods. Little money did she have, but little money did she need. She had no want for dainty morsels and spicy sauces. She preferred to live on milk, brown bread, broiled bacon, and now and then an egg or two. With this simple fare, she took good care of her two daughters, three hogs, three cows, and a sheep named Moll.

Now the old woman had a little yard enclosed with sticks and surrounded by a dry ditch. In this yard, she kept a rooster named Chanticleer. His comb was redder than the finest coral, his black bill shone like jet, his legs and toes were azure blue. His nails were whiter than a lily flower, and his neck and back were the color of burnished gold. Best of all, he had the loudest, merriest crow in all the land.

The noble Chanticleer took care of seven hens, the fairest of whom was named Pertelote. Pertelote was a modest and friendly hen. She carried herself well and sang beautifully. In fact, each morning, as the bright sun rose in the sky, Pertelote and Chanticleer sang in harmony, *"My Love Steps Through the Land."*

One day, as dawn broke, the sleeping Chanticleer began to groan.

Pertelote was aghast. She woke him and said, "What makes you groan this way, dear heart?"

"I dreamt I was in great distress, Madam," Chanticleer said. "My heart is still frightened."

"What did you dream?"

Many a lord
prefers a false
flatterer to one
who speaks the
truth.

"I dreamt that while I roamed our yard, I saw a beast who wanted to seize me and put me to death. His color was between yellow and red. His ears and tail were tipped with black. He had a long snout and two sparkling eyes."

"O, fie your chicken heart!" said Pertelote. "How can you fear a little dream? Did not a wise man say, 'Pay no attention to dreams'? I recommend that you eat some worms for your digestion."

"Madam, I believe that we should fear our dreams," said Chanticleer. "But let's talk of this no more. When I see the beauty of your face and the scarlet around your eyes, all my fears are banished."

Trying to salvage his pride, Chanticleer flew down from his perch and began strutting like a lion up and down the yard. When he found some kernels of corn, he clucked for his hens to come.

At that moment, a fox was hiding near the cottage. And when evening fell, the fox snuck through the stick fence into the yard where Chanticleer lived with his seven hens.

The fox hid in a bed of cabbages and waited.

The next morning, as Pertelote and all her sisters bathed in the sunlight, Chanticleer sang more merrily than a sea maid.

As the singing rooster gazed at a butterfly flitting among the vegetables, he saw the fox crouching near the cabbages. The fox's color was between yellow and red. His ears and tail were tipped with black. He had a long nose and two sparkling eyes.

"*Cok! Cok!*" Chanticleer cried, overcome with terror, for he recognized the beast from his dream.

He would have fled, but the fox blocked his path. "Gentle sir," the fox said in a kind voice, "where are you going?"

Horrified, Chanticleer could not answer as he stared at the fox.

"Are you afraid of a friend? I came only to listen to you sing, for you have a voice as lovely as an angel's."

The fox's flattery calmed Chanticleer down considerably.

The fox hurried on, "Your feeling for music is far finer than the greatest musician's. In fact, the only time I've ever heard a more beautiful voice was when I heard your own father sing. Please, sing now, and see if you can sing even more sweetly than he."

The fox's flattery made Chanticleer beat his wings with pleasure. Alas, many a lord prefers a false flatterer to one who speaks the truth.

The rooster stood high on his toes. He stretched out his neck and closed his eyes.

But as Chanticleer began to crow, the wicked fox leapt and seized him by the throat. Then he carried the rooster toward the woods.

All the hens shrieked with terror, and Pertelote, of course, cried the loudest.

The old widow and her daughters heard the hens. They rushed outdoors just in time to see the fox running toward the wood with Chanticleer in his mouth.

"Stop! Help!" they cried, and they ran after the fox.

All the neighbors picked up sticks and joined them. Yelling at the top of their lungs, they ran so fast their hearts nearly burst.

Dogs, hogs, cows, and calves ran, too. Ducks waddled. Geese flew over trees. Bees swarmed. Men blew trumpets and horns, until it seemed as if the very Heavens would fall.

Chanticleer, in spite of his terror, spoke to the fox. "Sir, if I were you," he said, "I would shout at that crowd chasing us. I would say, 'Turn back, all of you! As soon I reach the woods, I will eat this rooster! And there's nothing you can do about it!'"

The fox answered, "In faith, I shall do that."

As he opened his mouth to speak, Chanticleer fell from his jaws — then he flew high into a tree.

The fox was enraged. But he looked up at the rooster and spoke in a soothing, sweet voice, "Alas, O Chanticleer. I have wronged you. I made you afraid. I'm sorry. But I did it with no evil intention. Please come down, and I'll tell you what I really meant to do with you."

"Oh, no!" said Chanticleer. "You shall not trick me again with your flattery! Get me to sing and blink my eyes! He who blinks when he should see will never prosper!"

"And he who jabbers should hold his peace," growled the fox. And he slunk away into the woods.

*Those who consider this tale foolishness, as a tale only about a fox, a rooster, and a hen, should consider the moral for themselves. Everything is written for our own benefit.*

# NOTES ON THE STORIES

FINN MACCOUL — A race of people called Celts invaded Ireland in the fourth century B.C. For many centuries, the traditional stories of the Celts were passed down orally from one generation of storytellers to the next. But between the 1100s and 1400s, Christian monks wrote down the ancient Celtic tales in Old Irish. One of the most popular heroes of these Irish Celtic tales was Finn MacCoul. According to legend, Finn and his nomadic warriors, the Fianna, roamed the south of Ireland in the third century after Christ. The Finn stories began to be translated from Old Irish into English in the late 1700s. My retelling was mostly derived from one of the best-known translations, Lady Gregory's *Gods and Fighting Men*, published in 1904.

(The Old Irish quotation at the beginning of "Finn MacCoul" is from "Macgnimartha Find" in *Révue Celtique 5*. The English translation of the quotation is from *Fionn mac Cumhaill* by Daithi O Hogain.)

BEOWULF — When the Anglo-Saxons from the lands along the North Sea migrated onto Britain's shores in the early fifth and sixth centuries, they brought heroic tales about their ancestors with them. These stories, told in verse and handed down orally by poets, helped preserve the history of a people. One of the first stories to be written down tells about the warrior Beowulf, who saves the people of Denmark from a hideous monster. Beowulf is a Geat, a tribe of people who lived in southern Sweden. *Beowulf* is one of the oldest poems in Old English, the Germanic language of the Anglo-Saxons. It was written by an unknown poet and was probably fixed in written form between 800 and 1000. Translated into modern English in the early nineteenth century, *Beowulf* reflects the pagan, or pre-Christian, notion that immortality rests on heroic deeds. The name Beowulf is derived from "bee-wolf," or a wolf who raids beehives — hence, a bear.

*(The Old English quotation at the beginning of *Beowulf* is from *Beowulf,* author unknown. The English translation of the quotation is by Howell D. Chickering.)

THE SWORD IN THE STONE — After the Romans withdrew from Britain in 410, and the island was overrun by Anglo-Saxons from the Continent, legends sprang up about a Celtic-Roman leader who had resisted the invaders. His name was King Arthur. One of the first authors to write of him was Geoffrey of Monmouth in 1136. His book, *The History of the Kings of Britain,* was written in Latin. In the centuries that followed, Arthur was immortalized in many medieval romances. (The word *romance* was applied to stories written in French about knights and their deeds.) It has been said that half of all the finest masterpieces of medieval literature concern stories about King Arthur and his knights. In the 1450s and 1460s, Sir Thomas

Malory collected different Arthurian tales and translated them into Middle English. In 1485, Malory's book, *Le Morte Darthur*, was one of the first books published in English after the invention of the printing press.

(The Latin quotation at the beginning of "The Sword in the Stone" is from Geoffrey of Monmouth's *Historia Regum Britanniae*. The English translation of the quotation is by Lewis Thorpe.)

ISLAND OF THE LOST CHILDREN — In the thirteenth century, an unknown author compiled different elements from old German legends and wrote the epic poem *Gudrun*. Six hundred years later, the author's medieval manuscript was discovered in the imperial library of Vienna and translated into modern German from its original language of Middle High German. Since then, *Gudrun* has been regarded as one of the most valuable works of early German literature. The poem is told in three parts: The first tells the adventures of Hagen, the grandfather of Gudrun and the hero of the "Island of the Lost Children."

Since *Gudrun* is also mentioned in early Norse sagas, some scholars believe it may have been originally written in the language of Old Norse.

(The Middle High German quotation at the beginning of "Island of the Lost Children" is from *Gudrun*, author unknown. The English translation of the quotation is adapted from Mary Pickering Nichols.)

THE SONG OF ROLAND — *The Song of Roland* is the most famous hero tale of medieval France. It is the earliest example of a *"chanson de geste,"* or "a song of great deeds." Just as poets invented tales about the historical King Arthur, they also told hero tales about Charlemagne, or "Charles the Great." Charlemagne was a French king who, in the eighth century, led his army against those who did not practice Christianity, which included believers in the Scandinavian gods, Druids, and Muslims. Written probably between 1130 and 1170, *The Song of Roland* is the mythical account of Charlemagne's beloved nephew Roland who fought an Islamic army at the Battle of Roncesvalles in 777. In *The Song of Roland*, feudal honor and courage blend with Christian fidelity. Significantly, the story was written at a time when the nobles of Europe were heading to the East to fight a series of religious wars called the "Crusades," wars fought to win the Holy Land from the Muslims.

(The Old French quotation at the beginning of *The Song of Roland* is from *La Chanson De Roland*, author unknown. The English translation of the quotation is by Charles Scott Moncrieff.)

THE WEREWOLF — Many consider Marie de France to be the greatest woman author of the Middle Ages. Little is known about her, except that she was originally from France and was probably living in the English court in the late twelfth century. "The Werewolf" was written in Old French and comes from her collection of short tales called *lais* ("lays" in English), which are short romantic poems. The subject of werewolves held a great fascination for people of medieval times, as did the subject of love. This tale combines both in a parable about the forces of wild nature versus the forces of civilization.

(The Old French quotation at the beginning of "The Werewolf" is from *Les Lais de Marie de France* by Marie de France. The English translation of the quotation is by Eugene Mason.)

SIR GAWAIN AND THE GREEN KNIGHT — King Arthur's Knights of the Round Table followed the code of chivalry, which demanded loyalty to God, king, and one's ladylove, as well as courtesy, bravery, and honesty. During medieval times in England, France, and Germany, many tales were told about these honorable knights. One of the most popular was the poem of *Sir Gawain and the Green Knight*, written by an unknown English poet in the late fourteenth century. The poem reflects the medieval theme of testing the hero's honor under the threat of death.

*(The Middle English quotation at the beginning of *Sir Gawain and the Green Knight* is from *Sir Gawain and the Green Knight*, author unknown.)

ROBIN HOOD AND HIS MERRY MEN — During medieval times, a hero named Robin Hood was the subject of many English ballads, which were "poems meant for singing." It is not known whether Robin Hood actually lived, but his popularity as a legendary defender of the common people reflected the decline of absolute government power in England. For the last six hundred years, writers have continually remodeled Robin Hood and reimagined the tales of him and "his merry men" in songs, books, plays, and movies. My version is derived from Howard Pyle's immensely popular novel, *The Merry Adventures of Robin Hood*, written in 1883.

(The Middle English quotation at the beginning of "Robin Hood and His Merry Men" is from *A Gest of Robyn Hode*, composed in the 1400s, author unknown. The English translation of the quotation is by J. C. Holt.)

CHANTICLEER AND THE FOX — Geoffrey Chaucer is considered the first great English poet; and his most famous work, *The Canterbury Tales*, begun in 1386, is considered one of the greatest literary works of all time. Rather than write in the French or Latin language of earlier English writers, Chaucer wrote his masterpiece in Middle English, the common language of the people. The story celebrates the art of storytelling itself and gives a picture of the manners and morals of England in the late Middle Ages. One of its best-known witty tales, "The Nun's Priest's Tale," includes the story of "Chanticleer and the Fox," an example of a medieval beast fable, in which animals are personified to teach humans a moral lesson. The lesson in this story concerns the price of vanity.

(The Middle English quotation at the beginning of "Chanticleer and the Fox" is from *The Canterbury Tales* by Geoffrey Chaucer. The English translation of the quotation is by Vincent F. Hopper.)

*The opening quotations for *Beowulf* (page 8), and *Sir Gawain and the Green Knight* (page 50) were set with space between phrases to reflect their original sources. This literary convention follows a poetic pattern in which each line originally had two two-beat phrases, divided by a noticeable pause.

## Story Forms of Medieval Times

BALLAD — Poetry put to music and sung by troubadours and minstrels. "Robin Hood and His Merry Men" was first told in ballad form.

CHANSON DE GESTE — Early French epic, or a "song of great deeds," which reflects ideals of chivalry. *The Song of Roland* is the most famous *chanson de geste*.

FABLE — A story about legendary people (or animals) that makes a moral point. The story of "Chanticleer and the Fox" is an example of a fable.

HEROIC EPIC — A narrative poem that celebrates a real or legendary hero. *Gudrun*, the source of "Island of the Lost Children," and *Beowulf* are heroic epics.

LAY — A short romantic poem, not a song. "The Werewolf" was included in a collection of lays (*lais* in French) by Marie de France.

LEGEND — A story passed down orally from generation to generation about historical heroes. The story of "Finn MacCoul" is a famous Celtic legend of old Ireland.

ROMANCE — A story containing chivalry, mystery, and fantasy. These first appeared in Old French, a language derived from Latin (a "Roman" language, hence "romance"). "The Sword in the Stone" and *Sir Gawain and the Green Knight* are called Arthurian romances though their original sources include English and Latin writing.

## Some Early Peoples of Western Europe

CELTS — The Celts were Indo-European people who invaded parts of Europe, including the British Isles, in the fourth century B.C. They were dominated by priests called Druids and had a deep admiration for the power of words. When Britain was conquered by the Romans, the Celts withdrew to Wales and Cornwall. Escaping Roman rule altogether, Ireland kept Celtic traditions alive until the Irish converted to Christianity in the fifth century. Thereafter, Christian monks wrote down Celtic legends and history, and many Celtic influences found their way into the Christian faith. The Celtic language is the ancestor of Welsh and Irish Gaelic. Briton was the name of Celtic tribes discovered by Julius Caesar, thus the Romans called their island "Britannia."

ROMANS — After Roman soldiers conquered Britain in A.D. 43, the Romans dominated the island. They built Roman-style towns and roads and used Roman law and the language of Latin. At the time of the fall of the Roman empire in the fifth century, Roman legions were recalled from Britain, leaving way for the invasion of the Anglo-Saxon tribes.

ANGLO-SAXONS — "Anglo-Saxon" was the name given to Germanic tribes called the Angles, Saxons, and Jutes (from Holland, Germany, and Denmark) who invaded Britain in the fifth century. The word "English" comes from "Angle-ish." The Germanic dialects of Anglo-Saxon speech gave rise to Old English.

FRANKS — In the late fourth and fifth centuries, a Germanic people called the Franks overthrew the Romans in Gaul and established their own rule. Their land eventually came to be called France. They converted to Christianity and adopted the Roman language of Latin from which the language of Old French evolved. From 768 to 814, the Franks were led by Charlemagne, who was crowned Holy Roman Emperor.

VIKINGS — The Vikings were "fighting men" from Denmark, Norway, and Sweden who sailed to other lands, sometimes raiding and plundering them. They eventually settled in many parts of Europe, including Iceland.

NORMANS — Normans were Vikings who settled in northern France and adopted the French language, which had evolved from Latin. In 1066, led by William of Normandy, the Normans conquered England and for generations after, the English court spoke French.

# TIME PERIODS

DARK AGES — A name once used to describe the time between the fall of the Roman Empire and the Norman Conquest in England in 1066. Modern historians no longer use the term, as the period is more appreciated now for its important contributions to Western culture, such as the conversion of western Europe to Christianity and the preservation of classical learning, particularly in Ireland.

MEDIEVAL AGE — Also called the Middle Ages, the medieval period covered approximately a thousand years — from the time the Romans left Britain in the fifth century until the beginning of the European Renaissance in the fifteenth. Some historians consider the medieval period to be from the time of the Norman Conquest in 1066 to the fifteenth century, for they consider the Norman Conquest to be a turning point in European history.

RENAISSANCE — At the end of the fifteenth century the Renaissance began. The word "renaissance" means "rebirth," because of the rediscovery of the art, literature, and architecture of ancient Rome and Greece.

# WORDS RELATED TO MEDIEVAL TIMES

CHIVALRY — The word "chivalry" comes from the French "cheval," meaning "horse." Chivalry was a code of behavior for knights, or the horse-riding warriors of medieval times. Chivalry demanded valor, respect for women, protection of the poor, courtesy, and fairness.

CRUSADES — Starting in 1095, for two hundred years, knights from western Europe took a number of journeys to the Middle East to fight holy wars against followers of Islam. With the Crusades, medieval knighthood adopted a strong Christian identity, which is reflected in stories such as *The Song of Roland* and "The Sword in the Stone."

FEUDALISM — A form of social organization in which nobles gave land to vassals — other nobles or knights — in exchange for loyalty and military service. The feudal system governed all aspects of daily life.

KNIGHT — A medieval gentleman-soldier, usually a vassal.

LORD — A man of high rank in feudal society, such as a king or owner of a manor.

PAGE — A page was a young boy who lived in a noble's house and learned to fight and behave in a chivalrous fashion.

SQUIRE — A squire was a young man who served a knight and followed him into battle. If he proved himself worthy, a squire might someday become knighted himself.

TOURNAMENTS — Tournaments were specially organized fights in which knights practiced for battle.

VASSAL — A person who held land from a feudal lord and received protection in exchange for allegiance to that lord.

# THE EVOLUTION OF THE ENGLISH LANGUAGE

MODERN ENGLISH, the English we speak today, is made up of countless words from other languages. During the medieval period, it became mainly a mix of Germanic

Anglo-Saxon (or Old English), Latin (the language of Rome), and Old French (a language that evolved from Latin).

Anglo-Saxon, or Old English, was the Germanic tongue of the Anglo-Saxon invaders. The English language adopted Anglo-Saxon words to apply to the most basic aspects of everyday life. Words such as "life," "love," "work," and "death" are of Old English origin. Also borrowed from the Germanic language are words used for outer parts of the body, such as "arm," "nose," "hand," "finger," "eye," "ear," and "skin."

Latin, the language of ancient Italy, was often used for legal and religious matters. Words such as "felony," "justice," and "communion" are of Latin origin — though they may have come into English from French.

French, the language of the Franks that evolved from Latin, was often the source for words that indicated a more mannered and genteel way of life such as "courteous," "honor," and "noble." French-rooted words were also favored in cooking terms, hence "herb," "mustard," "poultry," "salad," and "lettuce." A character in Sir Walter Scott's *Ivanhoe* points out that we use the Anglo-Saxon-rooted words for livestock; for example, "ox," "calf," and "swine." And for cooked foods, we use the French-rooted words such as "beef," "veal," and "pork." French was also the source for words that describe many of the inner parts of the body, such as "vein," "nerve," "artery," "tendon," and "stomach."

# CHRONOLOGY

| | |
|---|---|
| Celts come to British Isles | 4th century B.C. |
| Romans conquer Britain | A.D. 43 |
| Finn MacCoul lives in Celtic Ireland | 200s |
| Roman legions leave Britain and return to Italy | 410 |
| Angles, Saxons, Jutes (collectively known as Anglo-Saxons) invade Britain from Germany | later 400s |
| Historical Beowulf may have lived and fought in Scandinavia | c. 500 |
| Historical King Arthur may have lived in Britain | c. 500 |
| Charlemagne (Charles the Great) led the Franks | 768–814 |
| Historical Roland may have fought for Charlemagne at Battle of Roncesvalles | 777 |
| Only known copy of *Beowulf* written down | c. 1000 |
| Normans conquer England | 1066 |
| Geoffrey of Monmouth writes *The History of the Kings of Britain* (which includes the story of Merlin) | 1136 |
| *The Song of Roland* written down | 1130–1170 |
| Marie de France writes "The Werewolf" | late 1100s |
| German epic *Gudrun* written down (which includes the story of Hagen) | 1200s |
| Ballads of Robin Hood first written down | 1300s |
| Geoffrey Chaucer begins writing *The Canterbury Tales* (which includes "Chanticleer and the Fox") | 1386 |
| *Sir Gawain and the Green Knight* written down | c. 1400 |
| Invention of the printing press by Gutenberg | c. 1450 |
| Sir Thomas Malory writes *Le Morte Darthur* (which includes "The Sword in the Stone") | 1450–60 |

# Artist's Note

THE COLORFUL SPECTRUM of medieval art created in Europe between the fifth and fifteenth centuries influenced my work for this book. The Middle Ages was a time of emergence from the classical antiquity of Rome and Greece; from the pagan tribal customs of the North; and from the mysticism of the Near East. It was a time of religion and superstition, of charity and brutality, of the mysterious and the mundane.

"The Werewolf" illustration alone reflects the essence of medieval thought and culture: the forces of darkness and light in the world and in the soul of man. This picture is also reminiscent of the "donor portrait" that was popular then. For this, individuals would hire artists to depict them in penitent or prayerful poses to show their piety and support for the church.

Throughout medieval art there are curious juxtapositions of fantasy and truth, saints and serpents, monsters and martyrs. Finding reference for my portrayal of the monster Grendel in *Beowulf* was easy. Monsters were everywhere — in stories, songs, art, and architecture. The bizarre creations of the late-medieval painters Bosch and Dürer served as my inspiration.

Architecture and art grew together during the Middle Ages, resulting in works of splendor and oddity. Cathedral ceilings celebrated the glory of the heavens, and stained-glass windows depicted biblical and allegorical scenes in a play of light and color. Grotesque and whimsical sculpted figures straddled buttresses and peered out of alcoves. As art found its way into architecture, architectural forms also found their way into art. In early illuminated manuscripts, figures were sometimes placed in an architectural framework or in a room with a cutaway view. Artistic scribes surrounded their depictions of kings and rulers with temple columns or castle archways on the manuscript page, as I have done in *Beowulf* and "The Sword in the Stone." Checkerboard-tile floors abounded in the architecture, similar to those that I have replicated in "The Sword in the Stone" and *Sir Gawain and the Green Knight*.

My composition for the *Sir Gawain* piece employs two other peculiarities of medieval art: the same characters appearing in different scenes within the same picture, and the graphic display of gore. Since martyrdom, beheadings, and torture were common during this time, it was not unusual for an artist to show blood spurting out of a person's side or headless neck.

In "Island of the Lost Children," the ornaments I used are based on twelfth- and thirteenth-century German initial capital letters. Artists would work a face or a scene into an initial letter and surround it with gold leaf. The basic colors used were blue, green, and various shades of red.

Color was sometimes symbolic: Red could stand for suffering, blue for charity, purple for royalty. In the Frankish kingdom of the great Charlemagne, costly purple dye, imported from Tyre, was used in many books, as was gold and silver leaf, which reflected the high standards of nobility. For *The Song of Roland*, I chose the colder look of silver to help capture the mood of the subject.

The format of this piece was modeled after the Lorsch Gospels, a book produced in Charlemagne's court. Blocks of type were divided into two columns, and because excellence in writing was a primary focus at this time, some of the finest letterforms came to be. Eye-pleasing, classically designed pages were the result. Colored lettering, too, was a trend, and in "The Sword in the Stone" illustration it adds a festive look.

My inspiration for the "Finn MacCoul" painting came from the Unicorn Tapestries. For the border around the text I referred to the Irish *Book of Durrow* and the eighth-century *Book of Kells*. Intricately interlaced lines known as Celtic knots and slithery doglike creatures fill these manuscripts.

The style of border framing the "Chanticleer and the Fox" scene became popular at the end of the fifteenth century. Though probably Flemish in origin, the practice of painting plants and flowers in borders spread throughout France and England. These borders present a wonderful world of botany in miniature along with an occasional insect. Small windows or tags on plants gave their Latin or common names. I have substituted these with a quote from the story. The flower here is the narcissus, representing Chanticleer's vanity. The fly, common to hen yards, adds to the earthiness of Chaucer's tale.

The border design for "Robin Hood and His Merry Men" was influenced by a late-fifteenth-century English psalter. Though my version of Robin Hood is not dressed in Lincoln green, I conveyed his legendary character by means of stature, stance, and a low horizon. The surrounding crowd, the castle turret, and the style of trees have the look of medieval art toward the end of the age.

The Middle Ages heralded the Age of Discovery. Meteorites showered the sky. Events were ordered by higher powers, and astrology flourished. I have chosen Merlin and the star-and-moon motif for the cover to represent the spirit of the day.

May the pages of this book open your eyes and mind a little wider — but most of all, may you enjoy.

*– Troy Howell –*

# BIBLIOGRAPHY

BAINES, KEITH (translator), *Le Morte Darthur*, by Sir Thomas Malory, New American Library, New York: 1962.

BULLFINCH, THOMAS, *The Age of Chivalry*, New American Library, New York: 1962.

BURGESS, GLYN, *The Song of Roland*, Penguin Books, England: 1990.

CHICKERING, HOWELL D. (translator), *Beowulf*, Doubleday, New York: 1977.

CLAIBORNE, ROBERT, *Our Marvelous Native Tongue*, Times Books, New York: 1983.

COOTE, STEPHEN, *English Literature of the Middle Ages*, Penguin Books, England: 1988.

GARDNER, JOHN (translator), *The Complete Works of the Gawain-Poet*, University of Chicago Press, Chicago: 1965.

GOODRICH, NORMA LORRE, *Medieval Myths*, Meridian, New York: 1994.

GREEN, DAVID H., *An Anthology of Irish Literature*, Modern Library, New York: 1954.

GUERBER, G. A., *Middle Ages*, Studio Editions, Ltd., London: 1993.

HOLT, J. C., *Robin Hood*, Thames and Hudson Ltd., London: 1982.

HOPPER, VINCENT F. (translator), *The Canterbury Tales*, by Geoffrey Chaucer, Barron's Educational Series, Inc., New York: 1948.

HUIZINGA, J., *The Waning of the Middle Ages*, Doubleday, New York: 1954.

MANCHESTER, WILLIAM, *A World Lit Only by Fire*, Little, Brown and Company, Boston: 1992.

MONCRIEFF, A. R. HOPE, *Romance & Legend of Chivalry*, Studio Editions, Ltd., London: 1994.

O HOGAIN, DAITHI, *Fionn mac Cumhaill: Images of the Gaelic Hero*, Gill and MacMillan, Dublin: 1988.

PYLE, HOWARD, *The Merry Adventures of Robin Hood*, Penguin Group, New York: 1985.

STONE, BRIAN (translator), *Sir Gawain and the Green Knight*, Penguin Books, London: 1959.

THORPE, LEWIS (translator), *The History of the Kings of Britain*, by Geoffrey of Monmouth, Penguin Classics, New York: 1966.

# INDEX